Birthing Hut AND OTHER STORIES

Birthing Hut and Other Stories

Thamizhachi Thangapandian

Translated by V Bharathi Harishankar

Vitasta

Published by
Renu Kaul Verma
Vitasta Publishing Pvt Ltd
2/15, Ansari Road, Daryaganj
New Delhi-110 002
info@vitastapublishing.com

ISBN 978-93-90961-75-7

First Edition 2022

MRP ₹350

Editorial Team: Alisha Verma, Manukriti
Cover and layout by Somesh Kumar Mishra
Printed at Chaman Enterprises, New Delhi

Contents

Foreword

I read Thamizhachi Thangapandian's short story, *The Stealthy Rain* in *Ananda Vikatan* recently. I felt that it's not a story one can read and move on. I have read it four more times since my first reading. The story, the choice of the theme, the tight plot structure and the language with which Thamizhachi has woven the narrative and above all, its aesthetic appeal—have made it a significant contribution to the Tamil short story canon.

The milieu of the story is an agrarian society, with people of the agricultural community as key players. The story unfolds from the point of view of

Periambalai, a common man belonging to this community. Vallimayil is his daughter. Then, there is Rasumagan, who is the sum total of petty thievery and mischief in the village. The people of the community including Periambalai are annoyed and angry with him. On that day, Periambalai spots Rasumagan as he leaves for the hay stack construction work. Vallimayil leaves home wearing a rose dupatta. Periambalai, full of scorn, curses Rasumagan and leaves for guarding the hay stack. Some bundles of hay have been stolen very deftly. Who is the culprit? In the dark, a figure moves on a bicycle with the stolen bundles. With a determination to bash up the culprit, Periambalai follows the figure, who enters the street where Rasumagan lives. The figure stacks the stolen bundles and switches on the light. Yes, it is Rasumagan. When Periambalai is ready to strike, he notices the rose dupatta around Rasumagan's neck. It is the same dupatta that Vallimayil had worn when she left the house in her youthful enthusiasm.

The story is not limited to this outline. Thamizhachi stacks different perceptions and uses innumerable spot lights to provide a kaleidoscopic view. Periambalai's affection towards his pregnant cow, his overwhelming affection for Vallimayil, the black sheep of a son, who tarnishes the image of an honest man Rasu, and Pattaiya—who unravels the etymology of the term 'stealthy rain'—Thamizhachi has used a limited number of characters to present the flavour of rural life.

There is no witness of the romantic relationship between Rasumagan and Vallimayil. It has not been described overtly. The aesthetic choice of the rose dupatta as an objective correlative of the romantic relationship is brilliant. This story points towards the offensive acts perpetrated in recent times by parents of girls who choose their own partners.

However, Thamizhachi has not stated the practice openly in the story but she makes every reader feel the pangs. She makes us recall those killings and makes us introspect our own emotions—making us confront the extent to which human perversion can reach. The understated tone is a definite literary victory for her.

Thamizhachi is a notable Tamil poet. Her collection, *Vanapechi*, captures the conscience of the Tamil people. Vanapechi feels bad when the plant in the neighbour's balcony wilts because it is not watered. It is clear that the story *The Stealthy Rain* has emerged from *Vanapechi's* soul.

Is this Thamizhachi's first story? Maybe. But, very soon, she will make her mark as a short story writer. I have no doubts regarding this.

—Thiru Prabanchan

Well-known Tamil Writer

Author's Note

All of us crave to listen to stories and this desire can even be attributed to the entire humankind. In the past, when civilizations were unfolding, the tradition of oral storytelling started from Homer's *Iliad* and *Odyssey*. Short versions, which could be told in one sitting, could be the precursor to what we read in one sitting today as short stories. But what we call a short story today came into existence in the nineteenth century. Walter Scott's story *The Two Drovers*, published in *Chronicles of the Canongate* in 1827, is arguably the first modern short story that was written. Incidentally, it is the English language that has produced this revolutionary genre. Following which different languages have produced innumerable iconic short story writers whose stories have changed the world. The distinguished list includes George Eliot, Thomas Hardy, Balzac, Alexander Pushkin, Ivan Turgenev, Fenimore Cooper, Nathaniel Hawthorne, Gustave Flaubert, Guy de Maupassant, Anton Chekhov, Edgar Allan Poe and Herman Melville among others. At home in Tamil, Puthumaipithan, Ki Rajanarayanan, Ka Naa Subramanyam, Ku Alagirisami, Jayakanthan, Prapanjan among others were some of the celebrated names that have inspired me all along.

It is a privilege and honor for me to have attempted this genre successfully and join the league of illustrious short story writers. This book was my first attempt outside the most comfortable zone of Poetry. It was critically acclaimed for its nativity, the 'Karisal' touch. For readers who are not familiar with Karisal, it is the region which I come from in Tamil Nadu, whose name is attributed to the type of soil. Most of the lexicons I have used here, hence are unfortunately termed as not so mainstream. However, I feel delighted to have recorded them, starting from my debut work. This is a deliberate and self-conscious decision in which I humbly try to pass on Karisal's petrichor to the next generation.

The five short stories individually published in various popular magazines were put together to give this book its current form. While the original Tamil work did not have any author's note, I write one today after almost three years of the original work published in Tamil, to send some strength and love for all the readers through the narratives found in these stories for the uncertain times that we live in.

This work originally titled *Muttu Veedu* in Tamil is very special, for being dedicated to the late Tamil literary doyen Prapanjan. A co-passenger in my literary journey and often a mentor, I am always grateful for the ample faith he had in me and my works.

It is assumed that anyone who is bilingual can do a competent translation. If it is the case, then anyone with the linguistic knowledge can carry out translation. It is much more than that because no two languages have common structure, syntax or vocabulary.

Known as the master translator of Modern Greek Poetry, Kimon Friar said, "Even the simplest word can never be rendered with its exact equivalent into another language." Often, the target language might not have an equivalent of the idea expressed in the source language. This is where a translator has to decipher what is said in the source language and deliberate how to reconstruct it in the target language without losing its nativity.

What is called word-for-word translation often fails to convey this; only a sense-to-sense translation alone achieves and thus prevails. As Mark Twain famously said, "The difference between the right word and the almost right word is really a large matter—it's the difference between lightning and a lightning bug." Hence, the process of translation is often termed as a negotiation between the two languages.

The images that one comes across here and the rich play of dialects are often very difficult to be delivered in English. I was very skeptical and did not initially concur to get this translated for its original rhythm would be lost. I am so glad that this has now seen the daylight, thanks to the illustrious Dr Bharathi Harishankar. Her most recent work, the English translation of the famous Tamil classic and one of my favorite reads, is *Nagammal.* A good friend and colleague whose work I admire and go back to often, she was kind enough to put this together for me. Thanks to her, *Birthing Hut and Other Stories* does not read like a literal translation. It is smooth to read and does not get 'Lost in Translation'. Even the title could have not been more apt than *Birthing Hut and Other Stories* for this collection, the reasons for which you will find after reading the book.

I hope that this is one of those opportunities for Karisal literature to be read and known by non-Tamil readers.

Happy reading!

—Dr T Sumathy

Translator's Note

Sumathy aka Thamizhachi Thangapandian is multifaceted and wears many hats with elan—Tamil poet, English Professor and a Member of Parliament. A common thread that runs through all these roles is a keen sense of observation, empathy and an enduring connect with people and places across the rural-urban divide. Thamizhachi is a well-established Tamil poet, who has published six volumes of poetry, all of which have represented the Karisal nativity, landscape and mindscape in its entirety.

Literature has provided a platform for our conversations over the last two decades. It has been an established practice between us that Sumathy would send me a copy of her publication, soon after it is published. My response would be to send a quick translation of the poem(s) that caught my attention in that collection. However, our desire to collaborate and bring out a bi-lingual volume did not materialise for various reasons. It gives me immense pleasure that Sumathy's short story collection has been successfully translated and brought out. Even though the 'new normal' existence has posed a lot of restrictions in terms of travelling and meeting people, it gave me the opportunity to traverse the textual space of the collection.

Muttu Veedu was one collection which spoke to me in the first instance and refused to be put away. As an individual born and raised in the city, the rural life captured in these stories took me back in time to the summers spent with grandparents in my native village. The urban life represented in these stories bring alive, not only the vagaries of an inconsequential existence, but also the extraordinary moments in the lives of ordinary individuals. The short story tradition in Tamil has a long list of such representations in writers like Pudumaipithan, Kumudini, R Chudamani to name a few.

As a translator, *Muttu Veedu*, demanded my attention in many ways. The language used in the stories certainly had the native flavour and to capture them in English was not an easy task. The Karisal tongue was intercepted effortlessly by the everyday urban usage. While the combination added unique flavours to the Tamil original, the translation had to negotiate the shifts and the nuances in a delicate and perceptive manner.

Texts are often termed untranslatable for different reasons. *Muttu Veedu* presented a scenario, where the form and content were deceptively simple. As a translator,

I was constantly concerned about making the English translation speak to the English-educated urban readers in the same way that the Tamil original talked to me. A glossary of terms has been included to provide a better understanding of the dialect used in the stories. There was an unintended outcome as well. The glossary provides an insight into the eco-poetics of the Karisal region, much in the spirit of the *thinai* classification.

—Dr Bharathi Harishankar

Translator's Acknowledgement

I would like to thank Sumathy for being a friend and entrusting the translation to me. The translation would have also not been possible without Thiru Prabanchan's perceptive foreword to the original text. Uyirmmai Pathippagam and Thiru Manushya Puthiran also played a major part for obtaining the permission to publish the Tamil original in translation, I will forever be indebted to them. Also, a big thank you to Mini Krishnan for suggesting me the possible avenues for publishing the translation. Last but not the least, my sincerest gratitude to Renu Kaul Verma for making the publication process easy.

Introduction

Birthing Hut and Other Stories is a collection of five short stories, namely *The Illiterate Wind*, *The Stealthy Rain*, *The Lotus Pond*, *Birthing Hut* and *Sleep*. Together, they evoke a landscape characteristic of the Karisal region in Tamil Nadu. The word Karisal refers to the black soil found in the Madurai and Ramanathapuram districts, which are rain dependent places. As if to compensate for the topographical inadequacy, the region displays a varied and vibrant culture.

The short stories in this collection effectively juxtapose the urbanscape of Chennai and the villages Nombakulam,

Sayalkudi and Naripaiyur. Such juxtaposition not only reveals the differences in places, but also showcases the people inhabiting the urban-rural divide. For example, *The Lotus Pond* contrasts the ostentations that mark a wedding in the city with a rural wedding of the narrator's paternal cousin.

> "Four wooden benches were arranged together and covered with a rug. Strings of marigold, which hung here and there were the only decoration .... Rural weddings emanate distinct smells – vicko turmeric and ponds powder from the ladies; the smell of liquor which cannot be contained by the small towel with which the men covered their mouths."

In contrast, the city wedding is a "package deal."

> "The stage was decorated in an elegant but understated fashion with

> lotus buds. No flashy zari* work .... As soon as we entered [the dining hall], a young woman held out a plate containing napkins .... Four well-dressed men occupied the designated seats. As they waited, one round of service was completed and a fresh set of disposable table covers was laid out .... Their faces showed no emotion."

The personal touch in the rural wedding, which brings the community together, is completely absent in the urban wedding.

The author peoples her narrative world with a wide array of characters. They are ordinary people with whom the readers are well-acquainted. However, they are etched with certain well-defined characteristics

---

* The meaning of the words with an asterisk is given at the end of the book.

that remain in our thoughts even after the stories have been read. As a rural person at heart, Periamma in *The Lotus Pond* is ill at ease in the urban setting. She's either withdrawn or reacting to the city culture. Kanna Anna in *The Illiterate Wind* is fifteen years older than the narrator but insists on calling her akka (elder sister). His simple justification is "how does it matter? She writes, speaks and teaches—let her be akka." Kombudhi Chinnamma* is obsessed with the idea of theetu or menstrual impurity. Ganesh with bouncing hair and handsome appearance succumbs to an untimely death due to the drinking habit. Pattaiya's extended story sessions impart life lessons. One memorable tale is that of the stealthy rain, which disrupts the hay stack work. To the query as to why the rain is called a thief, Pattaiya replies,

> "It not only spoils our work but also helps petty thieves. When we return the next day, the tarpaulin sheets

> would be in tact but some bundles would be missing. These thieves make quick bucks off our hard work. So, the rain gets the scolding for their stealth and thievery..."

What may appear as specific personality traits of individual characters actually serve to highlight the extraordinary aspects in the lives of ordinary characters.

The author captures with ease the extraordinary facets in characters through deep emotional moments. One such moment is reflected in Periambalai's feeling of helplessness when he comes to know about the relationship between his daughter, Vallimayil and the good-for-nothing loafer, Rasumagan.* Periambalai's original intention in following Rasumagan is to catch him red handed for stealing the hay stack bundles. He is determined to humiliate him in public.

"I'll yank his head off .... I'll expose his

theft in broad daylight and in front of the whole village. I'll spit on him, punch him and knock him out." However, "just as Periambalai was about to get up, he spotted the rose dupatta around Rasumagan's neck. Yes, it's the same dupatta that Vallimayil had put around her neck when she left for Sulochana's house." At this moment, his desire to humiliate Rasumagan is replaced by a sense of despair which "seemed as if a millstone had been placed on his chest." Through this simple phrase, the author captures Periambalai's emotional dilemma.

The sad news of Ganesh's untimely death brings on a surge of memories for the narrator. Her simple question to Jothi, Ganesh's wife, unleashes a powerful emotion that captures the plight of the young one year old bride:

> "Didn't you know that Ganesh had not returned home at night? If he had been found earlier, he could have been taken to the hospital and saved."

> "If yesterday was the first time he had returned late, I would have searched for him. It was a daily routine. Ever since the temple festival was announced…, he had had a gala time. I had sat up all night and gone to sleep when the cock crowed. I have not slept in the night for a year now."

Another narrative strategy that the author adopts is to present cross-sectional perceptions on a particular event. In the title story, the narrator and Azhageswari are unable to identify the strange smell emanating from the little hut:

> "This smell is familiar, is it not? Azhagu and I cried out in unison and breathed it in …. Then, we heard the crying of an infant. Azhagu immediately looked at her lap but the child was fast asleep. The elusive colostrum smell made sense to me now. It was the smell of a lactating mother."

This moment of discovery leads to very different reactions from Azhageswari and her mother Kombudhi Chinnamma, who had insisted that no food can be consumed from a house of the recently deceased and the newly born. While serving boiled sweet potatoes, the old lady informs that her granddaughter has recently delivered. It becomes of gratification and a fitting retort to Chinnamma's obsession about menstrual impurity.

> "Even though Azhagu and I didn't talk about it, we kept thinking about Chinnamma's reaction and exchanged smiles. It was gratifying that a sweet potato gave a fitting retort to her obsessive insistence on theetu and impurity."

In this collection, the author also dons the role of a narrator. Usually, this strategy limits the extent of the reader's perspective and freedom to traverse the text. However, in these stories, they introduce us to a close circle of characters across the urban-rural divide. Further, this twinning role of the author-narrator serves to connect with the readers in such a way that our judgement on characters and/or events are tempered and replaced with a deeper understanding. In some instances, it also brings in the surprise element as in *Birthing Hut*. Kamatchi Periamma's suicide and the visit to the mourning house set the context of the story. Azhageaswari has been forced by her mother to marry her uncle. All the events are set within these narrative axes. "When a husband slights the wife or abuses her in a forced marriage, the solution is not only to commit suicide but also to bear another child and bring a new life." In a flash, it highlights the loveless marriages of Periamma and Azhageswari and contrasts their differing responses to the similar situation.

There are several takeaways for the readers. On the one hand, the stories are tightly knit and present the depth of the narrative world. On the other, they spread a canvas on which different characters and their experiences are etched. Together, they enable a reading experience filled with sensitive emotions, pregnant silences and piercing realizations. This requires a self-assurance on the part of the writer about her narrative world and the words with which she crafts it. In my opinion, Sumathy weaves closely knit and intricate designs but also keeps her narrative world ensconced and safe in the palm of her hands. While reading and translating this collection of stories, I was constantly reminded of one of her recent poems written to commemorate her parents:

Asunam - Bird of Time

Like a lingering fragment
of yesterday's dream
weighs the tear drop
with an ocean's precipitate.

The iron spikes of sorrow
resound in the chattering teeth
as I lie helpless
like a storm battered tree.

The simmering loss
inflicts a searing wound of memory
like the sting of a scorpion.

"Appa" the call
rebounds from the void
to be heard in proximity.

The fond hug and cuddle,
the tender love in the rough cheek,
serene sleep and waking up
like a fresh blossom.

Is this an optical illusion
of the moonlight on the waves
rippling the surface with images?

Will a fleck of sand from the
mountain
dissipate in the hourglass of time?

Will the majesty
of the immortal voice
of Appa whispering into the ears
fade away?

With the warmth of the hand
unmoved by the termite of time,
with the cool tenderness pouring
into the fingertips,
with the twin border dhoti in place
and a breaking smile on the face
Appa embraces
Amma.

With the enduring warmth of
memories
to offset the searing cold
of the loss
the twin birds of time
Asunam
still nestle their
young ones.

—Dr Bharathi Harishankar

The Illiterate Wind

As I recall, I was in Harvest Organic Store when I heard the news. The gooseberries soaked in honey were so tempting that I was almost salivating. Ever since the Dubai dates have flooded the market and outnumbered the local varieties, it has become necessary to locate exclusive organic stores in Chennai. Amma* certifies that only Kandasami Annachi's* shop sells pure incense powder and authentic local dates. Whenever I see these dates, I remember Kannan Anna,* who used to suck the pips after eating the dates. As I put a packet of dates into the shopping basket, Ganesan called.

"Hmm. Okay. I'll come."

The lady who doled out the masala powder noticed the change in my expression but politely looked away. If this lady does not even sneeze while packing the powder, is this the genuine masala? This silly thought popped up and almost seemed natural, despite Ganesan's news. After paying the bill, I stepped out into the hot sun. I needed this heat and warmth to hit me. These are my crutches when I am homesick.

"Sumathi akka,* when did you come? Even yesterday, I read your poem in the diary."

"Anna .... it's not written by me."

"So what ... you read it out to me first. It struck a chord. So, it is your poem."

Chennai's searing heat kindled sweet

memories of this conversation. Still, I don't know why Sridharan was known as Kannan. He was older to me by fifteen years at least but insisted on calling me akka. The respect mingled with affection that poured forth when he called me akka certainly cannot be matched by the term Thangachi.* He felt that by calling me Thangachi, he was bossing over me.

"Kanna, Sumathi has literally grown up in front of you, why do you call her akka?" Mundiyanur Palmurugan would always ask.

"How does it matter? She writes, speaks and teaches—let her be akka" smiled Kannan in response showing his protruding teeth.

When he spoke to others, he would refer to me as "Sir's daughter."

"Anna, why do you introduce me that way? It's embarrassing."

If I sulked, he would hold my hands and say, "Sumathi akka, just for fun, okay."

That affection overrode the word fun.

When I reached home, I got busy in packing and buying the tickets. When I caught a glimpse of the actor Nagesh on the TV, Kannan Anna's memory gate crashed my mind. He was also slim like Nagesh and had a similar facial structure. Kannan Anna's memory refused to fade, like the lingering sweetness of the date seeds stuck in the molars. It was 10.30 in the night by the time I reached the village.

The main street in the village was still abuzz. Usually, people would have gone to sleep by 9 or 9.30 pm. The open doors of a house were silent listeners of the choicest abuses hurled by Kondal Raj's wife. Perhaps, Kondal Annan* was fully drunk and sprawled on the veranda.

"Tch, tch ... Ei, let us sleep in peace," said the old lady from the street corner.

That didn't stop the steady stream of shouts and expletives from Kondal Raj's wife.

Mahalingam mentioned that Kondal

Raj had picked up the drinking habit recently. Kannan Anna was a seasoned drinker. He never used to enter our house after drinking till my father was alive. After his death, I could find him sitting outside my room, fully drunk.

"What is this, Anna?"

"I should have died, when Appa* was gone."

A sudden bout of sorrow would burst forth through his tears and sleep deprived eyes.

"Have you eaten?"

"A little curd rice" replied Thottadri Iyengar's son, who always smeared the sacred ash on Kannan Anna's forehead.

In a rather plain and humble household, his games were part of my growing years.

"Even after reading that poem again and again, I don't get bored, Sumathi akka."

His eyes sparkled in the sunlight. In the yard filled with the smell of dried meat, he admired poetry without a frown.

His mother's name was Srivaramangai. He belonged to a conservative Vaishnavite family and worked as an assistant in the local school. He followed Appa like a shadow. No one knew how and why he picked up the drinking habit.

Once, in a fit of anger, I shouted:

"How can you pick up this deplorable habit? And, you give me lame excuses—Appa is not there … the goat is dead."

He didn't speak to me for a week.

"How can you equate Appa and a goat?" Fully drunk and standing outside the house, he shouted.

"Sumathi akka, did you arrive yesterday?"

With these words, he brought the fight to an end.

Things quietened. Perhaps, Kondal Raj and his wife have slept.

"Don't I have a name? Why do you refer to me as Kondal Raj's wife or as your sister-in-law?"

Her witty words and lilting tone are no longer heard and have morphed into a frustrated wife's angry and dinning words. Almost a day has passed since I received the call from Ganesan.

I woke up feeling humid and sweaty on the scruff of the neck. I could hear the cycle bells of children going to the Panchayat Board School and the clanging of vessels as Pandiamma washed them. I went down and sat on the backyard and waited for the karupatti kapi.* Maybe, Amma has gone to the temple. Where the salted and marinated meat was dried earlier, there were creepers of betel leaves now.

"He was alright when you came last month" said Kasturi akka and gave me coffee.

"Hmm … hmm ..."

I felt physically and mentally weighed down by sorrow and felt lethargic even to follow the routine of bathing and eating. After some time, I went to Kanna Anna's house.

Kala Manni* came and hugged me. Ananthu, Purani, Chemba, Lakshmi and Baby were all there. The house was filled with relatives. I spoke to each of them for a few minutes. Just hugged Lakshmi in silence. Minutes crawled and it was noon.

"We couldn't keep the body till you arrived. The temple has to be opened for the daily puja. When there is a death in Sannadhi theru*, even Chenna Kesava Perumal remains hungry," explained Venkatesh.

"No problem. I understand."

"Chitappa* wanted me to hand over this little bag with a parcel to you later. He had it on his bedside."

I received the yellow bag printed with information about the kumbabhishekam* of the Srirangam temple.

Oh, does 'later' mean this?

Kanna Anna's pet dog, which was circling around, jumped at the yellow bag. It had turned vegetarian for his sake.

"Do you feed curd rice to the dog as well?"

"Yes, after all, he's my sibling."

I stroked the dog, as it was trying to catch a whiff of his master's smell. I came outside and sat on the veranda.

Pandiamma, who always complained about the back breaking work of collecting the dried neem leaves there, sat next to me.

"Don't make a fuss, Pandiamma. The wind which scatters the leaves does not know how to read, he would say."

Pandiamma recalled Kanna Anna's words and started chewing her tobacco.

I opened the yellow bag. There was an old sheet of paper folded into four. In my handwriting from early college days were the lines.

"Do not pluck flowers
says the notice board but
flowers have been scattered
because
the wind does not know how to read."

I had copied the verse written on the grass near the Manimutharu falls by an anonymous writer. The word anonymous was erased and the name Sumathi akka was written. Along with it, there was one white slipper of my father.

"He nurtured this tree and the dog as his own" murmured Pandiamma.

"Both of them don't know how to read."

The wind stood still as we looked at each other.

*"Do not pluck flowers
says the notice board but
flowers have been scattered
because
the wind does not know
how to read."*

The Stealthy Rain

Periambalai barged in without even wiping the sweat pouring down his brows.

"Will you have some fermented rice water* (Neecha thanni)?" asked Pandiamma.

He paid no heed and entered the cow's enclosure. The cement water tub for the cow and calf was mostly empty.

"Mulish mule, sitting there without filling water," he muttered under his breath and splashed water on his face, arms and legs.

The ready-to-deliver Singhi sensed his presence and moved a little.

"Please be patient, my dear. Only three more days. Won't our Lakshmi come?"

The near human fatigue and discomfort of pregnancy were visible in the cow's appearance. He held it close and the cow heaved with the weight of the unborn. He lifted its tail and Singhi moved in sync.

"Ok ma … just a few more days."

He took a few ripe country bananas and fed the cow.

"Shameless fellow! Here I am waiting with the rice water and all your attention is on the cow" said Pandiamma.

He drank the fermented rice water in one gulp.

Noticing his starved stomach, Pandiamma said

"Ntha … looks like you are still hungry. Eat the remaining rice. I'll roast some dried fish."

She went into the room adjoining the enclosure. It was wet and musty. The small space included a corner for the kitchen, a cot in the middle and a clothesline at the other end.

"In all the 10-15 years we have been in this place for livelihood by constructing hay stacks, this useless rain has been a spoil sport."

Vallimayil was curled up on the floor, pretending to ignore Periambalai's lament.

"Get up. If you keep lying down, even the bare floor will warm up like a blanket."

Vallimayil turned a little on hearing Pandiamma's voice. For an instant, the near-term cow's face flashed before Periambalai. He shook his head in an attempt to clear the foolish thought.

The combined smell of the dirty clothes pile and the fried fish made Vallimayil even drowsier. Like a curled up cat, she tried to adjust her sleeping position but met her father's gaze and asked, "Who are you scolding now?"

Pandiamma entered carrying a velliyam* plate with hot rice, steaming tomato rasam* and fried fish. She nudged Vallimayil with her big toe and said, "Enough cuddling, get up."

At that moment, Singhi let out a low moan. On hearing this, Periambalai's hunger vanished and he pondered, "Poor thing! Till the burden is unloaded, it's a terrible experience for the female folk."

"Stop your musings. Only if the hunger is satisfied will the sweat of labour be enjoyable. Eat well."

Seeing that Vallimayil has still not got up, Pandiamma shouted irritably, "Useless bitch. Eats well and sleeps well. Get up! UP!"

Vallimayil got up reluctantly and cleaned the rheum in her eyes with her mother's sari pallu* She adjusted her long skirt and went to the inner yard. Husband and wife exchanged glances on hearing mill worker, Rasu's cycle bell. Rasu's son was a loafer, drunkard and a good for nothing fellow. Everyone knew how Rasu had to help him out of tricky situations. Their glance conveyed the fear of the offspring going astray.

Periambalai gargled his mouth and cleaned the plate. Looking at the sky, he cursed.

"Ass of a rain. Looks like it won't allow us to work on the hay stack construction. It is customary to gather the husk bundles in February and March after the harvest in January. But, year after year, a slow and steady drizzle would start at the same time and disrupt the post-harvest activities."

"That's why it's called the stealthy rain," Pattaiya had informed Periambalai.

Pattaiya was an expert in bedding the field and making grooves for sowing. Single handedly, he would get fifty-sixty of them ready in three hours. At eleven o'clock, he would drink his millet gruel with his grandson. Pattaiya's only concern was that his grandson didn't study beyond the fifth standard. Pattaiya would hold his large moustache to one side and drink his gruel. Periambalai would hand over the dried condiments and green chillies. Pattaiya's stories would begin with the first bite and envelop the paddy field, mountain and sky. Periambalai would be spell bound.

On one such occasion, the story of the Stealthy Rain took shape in response to Periambalai's question about its naming. Pattaiya took a bite of the spicy side dish and started:

"Deception is common but even that should have logic. This rain deceptively disrupts the work of the farmer. Thinking that barking dogs won't bite, we start work in the bright sunshine during the month of Maasi. We gather the husk, build a mound and return home thinking that we can tie up the hay stacks later. At 3 o' clock, like a little boy peeing on the thatched roof, a slight drizzle would start. Before we realise what is happening, there would be a downpour. Rushing across, we would cover the bundles in tarpaulin sheets and place heavy stones to prevent the sheets from flying off. At this moment, the sun would re-appear bright and hot. Always feel like using all the expletives on the rain."

"But why should we call it a thief?"

"It not only spoils our work but also helps the petty thieves. When we return the next day, the tarpaulin sheets would be intact but some bundles would be missing. These thieves make quick bucks off our hard work. So, the rain gets the scolding for their stealth and thievery as well."

When Pattaiya finished the story, not a drop of gruel would remain. He would rinse his mouth and drink a gulp of water from the stream.

Interspersed with stories, Pattaiya would also teach the intricacies of Padappai* (making hay stacks). Starting from a broad circumference, with single minded concentration, he would weave the bundles of husk into a pyramid. Periambalai always felt that Pattaiya's hay stack was a work of art, which surpassed the third standard drawing exercise of a house, sun, tree and mountain. Even now, if the drawing master hears about it, he may make him kneel down for the whole period.

Ever since, he started working as a youngster, Periambalai has been proud of his skills with the hay stack building and post-harvest work. He would stand guard and watch out for the stealthy rain and the thieves. Therefore, he was in demand.

Periambalai's reminiscences of Pattaiya were broken by the thought that the haystack work at the house with the arched entrance was only half completed.

"The rain has stopped. We can resume work" said Pandiamma.

At that moment, Vallimayil stood in front of him with a youthful glow. Brushing aside the thought, he looked at her from close quarters.

"What's it Appa?"

Vallimayil drew his attention by waving her hand.

"Where are you going?" he asked in response.

"Going to Sulochana akka's house to learn how to apply maruthani* design."

"Will you return quickly?"

"If you ask like this even before I step out, I need to run and sprint to her house and back."

"Ei, watch your words," admonished Pandiamma.

Vallimayil made faces at her as she adjusted her rose dupatta* and took out her bicycle.

"Will kill you, the..."

Periambalai also left.

"I have guard duty at the arched house tonight."

He wore his slippers and crossed the narrow thorny path to reach the main road. Like a short tempered wife, the sun was scorching.

"Let it remain this way till the work is completed." With this thought, he walked briskly.

Rasu's son, Rasumagan, came unsteadily in front of him. Periambalai quickened his pace to avoid him.

"Avoid the devil and it comes rushing towards you," he muttered.

Rasu's son rushed as if he would collide with Periambalai but swerved at the right time and kept ringing the bell as he rode away.

"What a show off! So much of dramatics on an empty stage!" said the lady from the neighbouring house and Periambalai nodded.

Pandiamma would react even on hearing the name of Rasumagan and cursed him wholeheartedly.

"A thorough rogue, who thinks he has the license to indulge in all bad habits."

Periambalai was puzzled over the appearance of Rasumagan, even after starting the work at the arched house. The drizzle started and he drew the tarpaulin sheet. He noticed a small dent in the haystack.

"Useless fellows … How insolent to remove the bundles even while I am on guard?"

Periambalai reached the grassland on the eastern side of the house where there was a clump of stinging nettles.

"Watch out what's in store for you, loafers."

Periambalai slid his hands into a plastic cover, plucked the nettles and put them in a jute bag.

"Edupatta payalugala,* this is how they ruin our livelihood. And this stealthy rain also acts as their accomplice. Let them so much as put a little finger on the hay stack now and face the sting and the itch," Periambalai swore as he placed the nettles.

"Of course, now I need to be careful while unpacking the stack. What a thankless job!" he mumbled.

After placing the nettles around the hay stack, he covered it with tarpaulin sheets and placed stones to keep them in place. By then, it was dusk.

Pandiamma had sent some millet stew with dried fish for the night through the chief mason. Scratching his own itching hands, he ate his dinner as the siren announcing the first shift in the mill rang. He dozed off only to be jerked awake by a dream. Vallimayil's cycle and Singhi's face floated before his eyes. It seemed as if the cow wore the rose dupatta. On hearing the sound of bicycle wheels, he closed his eyes and tried to determine the direction from which the sound emerged. It seemed to come from the northern end, behind the arched house.

"Let me catch the thief red handed."

Periambalai moved slowly and silently. He spotted the thief and the stolen hay bundles were on the carrier of the cycle.

"Let me find out how many bundles

he has stolen and where he's hiding them. It's surprising that he's not scratching and screaming even though the nettles must be stinging him. Must be a seasoned thief and he has to be handled with caution."

Periambalai followed the figure, who pried open the rear gate and rolled out his bicycle. The feeble light from the street lamps made things hazy.

"When have the Panchayat Board lights shone brightly?"

The figure with the bicycle entered the temple street and Periambalai realised that Rasu's house was there. He was furious at the thought that Rasumagan dared to steal when he was on guard.

"I'll yank his head off. Don't care even if it becomes a police case."

Periambalai entered the street with steely determination and eyes filled with vengeance. As he had predicted, the figure with the bicycle entered Rasu's house. In a flash, he also spotted the purple colour lungi worn by Rasumagan. Scratching his hands vigorously, the figure rushed to the well behind the house without even putting the stand for the bicycle.

For a moment Periambalai was raging to hit Rasu's son on the head but he controlled his fury.

"I'll expose his theft in broad daylight and in front of the whole village. I'll spit on him, punch him and knock him out."

He waited for five ... ten ... twenty seconds and hid himself in the hen coop. No doubt at all, it was Rasumagan.

Making sure that no one had noticed or followed him, Rasumagan turned on the light in the veranda. Just as Periambalai was about to get up, he spotted the rose dupatta around Rasumagan's neck. Yes, it's the same dupatta that Vallimayil had put around her neck when she left for Sulochana's house. Periambalai felt faint. It seemed as if a millstone had been placed on his chest. He was too dazed but caught himself watching

Rasumagan smelling and spreading the dupatta over himself. Periambalai choked and could hardly breathe. An apparition with Singhi's face and Vallimayil's body floated before his eyes and seemed to mock him. He felt claustrophobic.

Periambalai stood in a daze, unaware of when Rasumagan switched off the light and went to sleep. Hearing the morning sounds, he came back to his senses and came out of the coop. He put the bicycle of Rasu's son in its proper place. Even now, Periambalai could sense that Rasumagan had covered his lust-filled face with the rose dupatta. He made sure that he had put the hen coop basket in place and silently walked back to the arched house.

"Would those nettles be still stuck in the rose dupatta?"

Thinking thus, he opened the wooden rear gate to the arched house.

The Lotus Pond

We entered the marriage hall, even as Periamma* wondered aloud why so many young women were crowding the entrance. The women wore colour coordinated dress, smiled a little, greeted and sprinkled rose water. As we walked in, tasting a little sugar candy, a toddler in a blue sharara* tripped and fell. Periamma hitched up the dress saying, "now it will not trip her up." The toddler's mother said thanks but pulled down the skirt. Periamma was crestfallen. When she first came to Chennai, she would react to everything but now she has got used to things to such an extent that she does not even worry about the ever increasing rates of aavin milk. This sudden reaction is a rarity now. Ignoring this, as I was searching for a place to sit, an acquaintance guided us to the front row. Even though he looked familiar, his name eluded me. As I was searching for words to utter some pleasantries, he moved away to greet other guests. Perhaps, I was over enthusiastic in my attempt to recall his name.

Photographers were literally sprawled on the floor to capture the child in blue skirt. With a smug look full of pride, the mother adjusted the dupatta rolled into a ball by the child and at the same time ensured that she was also in the frame. There were several delicacies on display and the boy in pyjama kurta was busy eyeing the joker face cake. The stage was decorated in an elegant but understated fashion with lotus buds. No flashy zari work. I curtailed an old fashioned thought that crept in.

"The unblossomed buds hung
with the thoughts of
blossoming in the pond
tomorrow."

In its place, came a nonsense verse.

"The fully blossomed lotuses
took a selfie – the buds."

I put a stop to these rambling thoughts and looked at Periamma. She sat tight lipped in an effort to stop all questions and looked at the crowd absentmindedly. After ten minutes or so, I asked her "Shall we go on the stage to greet the couple?"

"The TV monitors are showing them very clearly. Do we need to go up?" she demurred, but got up to avoid my stern look.

I was reminded of the wedding of my paternal cousin from Nombakulam village that took place last month. Four wooden benches were arranged together and covered with a jamakkaalam.* Strings of marigold, which hung here and there were the only decoration. The wafting smell of beef curry beckoned even the Nagaswaram players. They tilted towards the smell even as they were imploring Lord Muruga. After distribution, the leftover kadambam* flowers were spread out on a large plate.

Even as the Rattha poriyal,* a delicacy made out of fried goat's blood seasoned with spices, was being cooked, some kids tasted it. To avoid anyone detecting their act, they dunked their hands into the bowl of sandalwood paste. All this subterfuge was only to ensure that they got another share of the delicacy. Rural weddings emanate distinct smells—vicko turmeric and ponds powder from the ladies, the smell of liquor which cannot be contained by the small towel with which the men covered their mouths. Such distinct smells cannot be found in city marriage halls.

"Don't stamp on the lotus bud," Periamma tapped my shoulder and alerted me.

For the people from the black soil region, lotus is a rare occurrence and so is water.

Someone came and took us ahead of the waiting queue. As I handed over the bouquet, Periamma was looking for kumkum* and atchadai* to bless the couple.

"Others are waiting. Let's go."

I felt bad, even as I rushed her.

"Haven't even seen the faces of the bride and groom properly" muttered Periamma.

The dining hall, with its heavy crowd, looked like a misshapen bean bag. The gentleman who took us to greet the newlyweds, helped us now as well. Sensing my hesitation, he said, "Don't worry. I have asked some of our boys to hold a few seats."

On seeing him, a few women—may be servers or helpers—got up hurriedly. As soon as we entered, a young woman held out a plate containing napkins, Periamma and I looked at each other. Our thoughts echoed: "A plate containing napkins could have been placed on a stool. What's the need for a young woman?"

As we neared the dining tables, unable to hold her thoughts, Periamma blurted out, "What a spectacle! Did you see?"

It was an uncomfortable sight. Four well-dressed men occupied the designated seats. As they waited, one round of service was completed and a fresh set of disposable table covers was laid out. At that moment, I also noticed that the man who accompanied us wore a 'safari suit'—an apparel which makes the wearer look and feel like a gentleman. On seeing him, the four men stood up but he motioned them to hold till the serving was completed. Their faces showed no emotion.

"No problem. Let them finish eating" Periamma said.

"They are holding the seats for us", I whispered.

I was not sure that she understood the concept but the smile on her face had totally vanished.

When the new leaf plates were placed, the young men made way for us and responded with a curt nod to my thanks. They had been trained well and did not reveal the fatigue or boredom and kept their forced smile intact. They shifted and moved on to hold seats for others. We started eating. Periamma ate very little (for formality) and even her pasted polite smile had vanished. Even after we finished eating, we noticed that the youngsters were still holding seats. One of them walked before us and hastily, I smiled and said "sorry." It appeared as if he hadn't noticed. Periamma refused to take the napkin from the young woman and wiped her wet hands on her sari pallu. Without exchanging a word, we took leave amidst the loud noise and left the marriage hall.

At the entrance, we waited for the driver to pick us up. Periamma drew my attention to the cramped space under the staircase. One of the youngsters who held our seats opened a parcel hurriedly. The hunger in his eyes didn't match his sophisticated dress. The smell of the chutney* merged with the musty smell and made me nauseous.

Periamma and I didn't utter a word, even after we got into the car. We went past the entrance and sped over a little bridge. Periamma opened her sari folds and took the lotus bud. I thought she had liked it and brought it along.

"He keeps waiting before the serving rows and eats out of a parcel. Why do I need this meaningless thing?"

She threw it out. Like an unpleasant dream, the Cooum River* received the lotus bud.

Birthing Hut

The twinning snake gourds became the flailing arms of the mourners. Blood spurt out from the veins. Many hands strangled my neck and made me voluptuous but I felt no fear. The faces of the hugging mourners were facing behind and out of them the long extended tongues sprawled across the floor. They licked and sucked the flowing blood and spurt it over the head. Two of the drops fell on my neck and flowed down and coloured the nipples red. The suckling infant turned and whined. There was a streak of blood in the corner of its mouth and a fully grown moustache.

I broke into a sweat and woke up with a start. Even though my conscious mind confirmed that it was only a dream, I involuntarily muttered, "Where's the one sided moustache?"

Azhageswari pinched me and asked, "Daydream, is it? The car has stopped in these back woods and you are searching for the one sided moustache?"

I was terrible embarrassed. I wiped my face. By then, she had buttoned her blouse and adjusted her sari folds. She held the sleeping child in an awkward position between her shoulder and hip. The Cuticura powder had mixed with sweat and formed white streaks on the nape. The smell of dry ginger on the child's hands and the lingering colostrum in the corner of its mouth gave a pleasant breath in that sultry surrounding.

Since it was rather congested with five people in the back seat, Kombudhi Chinamma and Azhageswari's husband had got down from the car. Her elder daughter, Srilekha, was busy blowing air into the empty Lays Chips packets and bursting them. Since I had dozed off soon after we left Sayalkudi, I was unable to locate why and where the car had stopped. Adjusting my sweaty limbs, I got out of the car.

"Ei Lekha, get down."

Azhageswari also got down with the infant.

"Where are your slippers, Azhagu?"

"I never wear slippers to a mourning house because they would surely get stolen."

Her husband was smoking at a distance. Chinamma's irritation was evident in the way she splashed water out of the bottle on her face. Keeping pace with her, Kombudhi Chitappa, who had comfortably sat alone in the front seat, also moistened the turkish towel and wiped himself.

"What a bother! We are stuck in this place. Perhaps, we should have eaten something before we left" he said.

"How can we cook after hearing about the death?" Chinamma scowled.

Her large vermilion pottu* was partly washed away and stuck in Chitappa's turkish towel. We can never spot her without the large pottu.

"Usually, I carry the chenthurukka dabba* and ambarai.* Since we left in a hurry, I forgot to pack them," said Chinamma.

"Please hold her for a while."

Azhagu handed over the six month old infant and walked towards me.

"I need to use the toilet, my bladder is full. Where can we find a secluded spot?"

I was in a similar predicament.

It was only when we looked for a secluded spot did it struck us that it was a sparsely fertile low land. Pandian, the driver, was nowhere in sight. Looking at the babul shrubs on a slope, we walked a little. Lekha Kutty hopped behind us.

"This doesn't look like the main road. We were looking for a short cut to reach Parthibanur, but the driver has brought us on this thorny path and punctured the tyres."

As she spoke, Azhagu knotted her hair. Even then, her sari pallu was sprawled and not gathered.

"Why are you staring at my chest? I have gotten used to having it open. He scolds me saying that this is an open invitation to the whole town. Hmm ... With these sagging breasts, what sensual feast can I offer?"

Azhagu looked like a veritable line drawing of dejection. The memory of a younger Azhagu with matching ribbon, bangles and sticker pottu, draped in the latest design Madurai or Virudhunagar sari and walking with her jingling anklets during the car festival flashed before me. Now she wore no jewels except for a small earring and the thali* chain.

"My leg is aching. Please carry me," said Lekha Kutty.

Azhagu smacked the girl on the back and the child sat on the mud track and started crying.

"You ignore her and keep walking. She'll follow. I need to pass urine urgently."

She pointed to a spot where there were two babul trees and some aloe vera plants. As we squatted, she said, "I met Mani. He has put on some weight and looks handsome."

Without answering, I thrust the water bottle.

"His wife also cooks tasty pirandai* chutney and dried fish sambar.* He had also brought some milk buns for me."

"Did he come? When? Where?"

Without answering, she returned the water bottle.

When we reached the spot where the car stood, we saw Azhagu's husband playing with Lekha Kutty. Chinamma and Chitappa sat on a felled pine tree and were talking loudly. She had put Aishwarya Pappa* on the back seat of the car. I checked and made sure that the car doors were open.

"Have you emptied the whole bottle? You have made me sit in this no man's land and I haven't had a head wash after the mourning visit. I am trying my best not to urinate because we need water."

On his part, Chitappa muttered his complaint.

"She and her theetu* nonsense. She prevented us from eating anything in the mourning house and didn't allow us to eat at home before we left. I am ravenous. If I don't eat, how can I feed the child?"

Mother and daughter were always at logger heads. Chinamma had doused herself in kerosene and threatened to commit suicide in order to make Azhagu marry her brother who was 15 years older.

There was no sign of the driver. Aishwarya Pappa started crying. Azhagu banged the car door and started feeding her.

"Arrogant bitch. This shrew has not been tamed even after the marriage. She'll ruin my brother's life."

Chitappa gave her a stern look.

Periamma continued,

"The man sitting in the front seat should guide the driver. He's from the city. How can we expect him to know the short cuts?"

"No Chinamma, he's an experienced driver. I didn't expect him to come without a stepney," I answered.

"Amma. I am very hungry."

Lekha Kutty came running. On seeing Chinamma's fury, I drew her near me. I felt that it was a good thing that I had offered to drop them on the way. Sensing my thoughts, Chitappa said, "It's good that we travelled together. Otherwise, you would have been stranded all alone."

I knew I could call Pandi and enquire where he was, but I didn't feel like it. I liked the narrow path away from the din of the main road. Unlike the others, I was not bored. As an observer, I have gotten a chance to witness Chinamma's anger, the crying infant and Azhagu with her hair in a top knot. With his lungi hitched up, Azhagu's husband came and without looking at anyone in particular, announced:

"I'll walk up to the main road and look out for other vehicles."

He completely ignored Chinamma's facial cue asking him to unfold his lungi.

"Appa, I'll also come."

No one seemed to either listen to or console Lekha Kutty. I sensed her hunger induced tears and made her sit in the front seat.

With her mouth ajar, Azhagu had fallen asleep in the back seat. Her unbuttoned blouse that let the breeze in, her tired face, the sleeping infant, the mild noise of suckling—all spread a warm glow in contrast to the deathly pallor at the mourning house.

"I can hear the ice cream van, Periamma."

Lekha Kutty jumped out of the car and Chitappa came in time to hold her.

My head started throbbing due to the hunger. Suddenly, the smell of Kamatchi Periamma burping after a meal of mutton gravy enveloped the car. It was still difficult to understand why she consumed pesticide and died. I have always thought of her as a contented person in a Madurai sungudi sari,* with a string of jasmine around her bun hairdo, betel leaves in her mouth and a connoisseur of non-vegetarian food. She had never complained about marrying Koduvanthan Chitappa or the fact that he lived in Singapore while she stayed back in Sayalkudi.

"These feather like and transparent

saris are for youngsters like you."

I still remember the one in lavender colour with a white border. It has remained my favourite and I always felt that I could smell Kamatchi Periamma's burp rather than the napthalene balls. Whenever I teased her about her golden tooth, she would retort, "The smile and the laughter remains in Singapore and only the tooth remains here."

I had a severe headache. It felt like someone was banging my forehead with a hammer. The sultry heat intensified the pain. In an irritable moment, I said, "Wake up, Azhagu."

Sensing the harsh tone, she woke up in a hurry, buttoned her blouse and asked, "Is it over?"

The child on her shoulder burped just then and the smell of Kamatchi Periamma's mutton biryani filled the car. Without uttering a word, I got out of the car and banged the door.

"Are you taking turns to get the car door off its hinges?"

Kombudi Chinamma got up and adjusted her sweat drenched petticoat which had left a circular spot on the pine log.

"Had we gone by bus instead of accompanying you, we would have reached home by now, bathed and gotten rid of the ritual pollution."

Azhagu intercepted her.

"You speak as if you were born and married into households where no one has ever died. You are obsessed about this theetu business. Were you born without the menstrual blood?"

Kombudi Chinamma got furious and shouted, "It's my mistake that I allowed you to study. Yes, there is impurity in the birthing hut and the mourning house. I will not eat in either place for thirty days."

"Will you follow this practice even if your husband dies?"

"Yes bitch, even if your husband dies."

"Remember, my husband is your thombi,* your little brother."

"Yes, now you remember that my husband is your father."

"If that's your stand, take an oath on Pechiyatha."*

Before Azhagu completed her sentence, Chinamma caught hold of her hair and slapped her hard on the back. In the vision of my hunger pangs, they appeared to be like two cobras in fight. Since the two were always at loggerheads, Chitappa ignored them and came up at a leisurely pace from behind the babul trees.

"Chinamma, stop the fight …. Ei, Azhagu, stop..."

My words were drowned by the cry. I glared at Azhagu and took the child.

"I have not eaten anything after drinking the gruel yesterday night. If this kid keeps suckling, will any milk come?"

Azhagu reached out to hit the child and her hunger was evident in her reddened eyes.

As I opened the car to call the driver, the child started screeching. I patted the child on the back, pacified it and closed the door without taking my mobile.

"Aatha,* I can spot a hut in the middle of the pine grove. If we go there, we'll at least get some water and buttermilk. Let Pandi come later. You take your bag."

Chitappa spoke and started walking without waiting for our response. Even as I wondered where Lekha Kutty and Azhagu's husband were, I saw them at a distance. He was carrying the child and her ribbon was bobbing in the wind.

"Appa, don't press my anklet."

Her strong voice indicated that she had eaten something.

I started walking and assumed that Azhagu will bring my bag. Even though the mother and daughter did not utter a word, their steps echoed their anger and hunger. Even without looking back, it was clear from the jingling sound of Lekha

Kutty's anklet that she and her father were behind us. After walking for about twenty minutes, we spotted a thatched house adjacent to the motor room. Seven or eight pine trees surrounded the house, like tall women with unruly hair and their saris hitched up to reveal their thighs. When Chitappa opened the gate near the fence, a garden lizard slid past and he called out,

"Eppe, who's there?"

Beyond the fence was a string cot. At the end of a low veranda was a door made of tin sheet, which was half open in a slanted manner. Chitappa went behind the house looking for people of the house. Azhagu and Chinamma sat on opposite sides of the veranda, each propped against a pillar. On seeing her mother, Lekha Kutty ran to her. The place was full of goat droppings and two woven palm fronds provided shade to the string cot. I sat on it and put the child on my lap. The musty smell from the goat poop combined with a milky smell rekindled my hunger.

"A frail, old woman was lying in the backyard and I have asked her to come," informed Chitappa in a tone which revealed his hunger and frustration.

Chinamma and Azhagu were so fatigued that they couldn't even fight.

"Thatha, I am very thirsty," said Lekha Kutty and hugged him.

"Then, go and jump into the well," he scowled.

Lekha Kutty retracted in fear and snuggled close to me. Azhagu's husband looked the other way and was aimlessly scratching the pine tree.

The makeshift tin sheet door opened and a hunched old lady literally crawled her way out.

"Come in, Thayi,"* she welcomed in a loud voice.

She was so frail as if she would crumble into powder but her voice was loud and strong. Azhagu read my thoughts and we exchanged sidelong glances and smiles. All three of us went in and it took a while for us to get adjusted to the darkness. A large room was divided into two and the inner room was closed. There was a fire place and some kitchen utensils in the corner. There was also a clothesline in the middle of the room with a few dhotis,* free saris distributed in ration shops and some dirty towels. A strange smell of fresh meat wafted but I was unable to spot it even though I took a deep breath. I looked at Azhagu and her nostrils had flared up. Most likely, Chinamma must have asked for the toilet as the old lady had taken her to the backyard.

"This smell is familiar, is it not?"

Azhagu and I cried out in unison and breathed it in.

Azhagu took back the infant from me, as it was craving for milk. Even after we sat down, we were unable to locate the smell. The old lady crawled in like a centipede after the rain and took out two velliyam plates and rinsed them. She brought two large glasses of buttermilk.

"We have only two plates," she said and placed some boiled sweet potatoes. She put one plate before us and took the other for the men waiting outside.

We ate in silence since it would have been impolite to enquire about the other members when the old lady had not broached the topic. Even though we couldn't make eye contact with the old lady because of her hunched back, it was clear that she kept glancing towards the inner room.

"Shall I make some ragi porridge?" she asked.

"No, we will leave now."

Then, we heard the crying of an infant. Azhagu immediately looked at her lap but the child was fast asleep. The elusive colostrum smell made sense to me now. It was the smell of a lactating mother.

"May you live long! Only now, I feel alive. Sweet potatoes are wholesome and we can manage till we reach home and bathe," Chinamma said as she entered.

"My granddaughter had her delivery three days back. Her mother has gone to Kamudhi to buy things and her husband has gone to pay the electricity bill. That's why I am unable to cook anything elaborate in this birthing hut."

Kombudhi Chinamma's face lost colour and her adam's apple bobbed with emotion. Her eyes narrowed and lips were pursed tightly. She got up hurriedly and pried open the makeshift door.

"Please do it softly, aatha. The new mother is fast asleep," said the old woman.

"Please put the sacred ash on my forehead and bless me, Paati,"* asked Azhagu.

"Oh, you spotted the sacred ash tied in the sari end," exclaimed the old woman and smiled.

She accompanied us till the fence. Chitappa walked in front and Azhagu's husband was carrying Lekha Kutty. Chinamma walked behind them and the heaving of her chest was quite visible even from behind. As we stepped out, I asked,

"Is it a girl or a boy?"

"Pechiyatha has come," she replied.

Even though Azhagu and I didn't talk about it, we kept thinking about Chinamma's reaction and exchanged smiles. It was gratifying that a sweet potato gave a fitting retort to her obsessive insistence on theetu and impurity.

Pandi had fixed the stepney tyre and gave an artificial smile to respond to our angry queries. Only Chitappa muttered something to him. Azhagu's husband took two more cigarettes from the driver and got into the back seat. Chinamma was already inside and her hungry face was replaced by a crestfallen countenance. While Azhagu's husband stood aside to let me get in first, she whispered, "When the husband slights the wife or abuses her in a forced marriage, the solution is not only to commit suicide but also to bear another child and bring a new life."

"Is that so?" I looked at her.

"Mani has a large mole above his right knee," she said as she hurried me into the car.

I sat next to Periamma and held out my hand to take the little child. It willingly rushed into my arms and there was a large mole above its right knee. Azhagu, her husband and Lekha Kutty got in and Pandi started the car. Azhagu and I snuggled close and were enveloped by the smell of sweet potatoes and breast milk.

Sleep

I heard the news when I was in the book shop. Even though, I resolve to buy new books only after reading the previous lot, my hand involuntarily reaches out to pick a new book. Perhaps, I feel satisfied only when I see them stacked in my own book shelf.

"Hmm … I have started."

I answered the mobile and moved towards the car. I walked past a young man in dirty jeans and T-shirt. He didn't notice me, but kick started his bike in a hurry.

"Why haven't you worn a helmet?" I muttered.

He shrugged off this question from a stranger. My eyes brimmed with tears when I got into the car. The ever conscious mind had prevented the eyes from shedding tears in public. It was frustrating that Chennai was fast paced even at 9.30 pm.

Ganesh was more or less the same age as the young man on the bike. Why did he do this? Why did he go out yesterday night? With every question, my eyes misted.

"Why were you not named Pandian—Piping Pandian?"

I would tease him about his smoking habit. Even though he pretended to ignore the comment, he would clam up.

"Akka, how can you say this? Who feeds you with this pack of lies?"

When he swore this way, I would warn him against making false promises.

"Ayyo,* akka. I am the eldest, only son. Will I do that?"

As he spoke animatedly, his hair would bounce beautifully. Ganesh was quite proud of his thick curly hair.

"No need to flaunt. Whoever eats a lot of fish would have such hair."

"Kidathirukkai Boopathi is my age and even dreams of dried fish in his sleep, but one can play a good Kittipul* (tip cat game) on his bald head," he would retort.

Tension mounted. I returned home and started packing. I have to pick up Amma enroute at Madurai. Naripaiyur is three hours' drive from there. It would be noon by the time I reached.

"Night time. Drive carefully."

Mama's* words made Mariyappan a little tense. He sat uncomfortably till I got in. In my distraction, I had completely forgotten the wound on my dog's back.

"Take care of Kushi."

My voice burst out a little too loudly.

On hearing its name, the dog rushed towards me but I had already got into the car.

"Poor soul. Very young."

Muniyamma's words echoed. She didn't mention the name—did she refer to Ganesh or his bride of one year, Jothi? Thoughts clamoured. I couldn't even read a book. I should have cried when I was alone. The haste to leave on time had gobbled up the tears.

The never ending SMS, text messages and Pongal greetings were bothersome. So, I switched off my mobile. Ganesh and Jothi had got married in a theatre in Naripaiyur. Face flushed with joy and excitement, she had stood near him. Ganesh was all smiles and couldn't take his eyes off her. He had even offered his handkerchief for her to wipe the sweat, which made her even shyer. Picture perfect moments.

I reached Madurai. On Amma's insistence, I bathed and quickly ate a few bananas. As we drove to Naripaiyur, Amma kept talking about Ganesh. It seems he hadn't returned home till early morning and that's when they had started searching for him. Without any reason, Jothi's face flashed before my eyes. Amma dozed off but I felt queasy and uncomfortable. As we entered the street Thachanendhal, where Ganesh used to live, Mama stopped us and said, "Not here. It's kept in the street corner."

The place was crowded. Chitappa and Chinamma were inconsolable. Kamatchi Patti and Poovarasi broke into a dirge. With a hardened face, Jothi sat in the middle. Is she crying or has she exhausted her tears? In the middle of the street, the corpse shrouded in white was laid.

The cries reached a crescendo. I sat near the mangled and shrouded body.

"Since post mortem was done, we couldn't take the body home. Poor girl, she can't even mourn in private."

On hearing Chinamma's words, the crowd burst into tears.

"He has tattooed your name on his left hand. It's intact. I saw it," Jothi whispered.

The pent up tears swelled and I broke down.

Only after all the rituals were completed the next day, I could speak to Jothi in private. She had cleaned the house and washed her hair. I could spot a baby bump but stopped myself from asking her. She brought a jug of black coffee and sat next to me. Her swollen eyes revealed her sorrow and sleeplessness. As I sipped the coffee, I felt hungry. Sensing it, she brought some milk buns. I gave her a piece and she started chewing it slowly.

"Didn't you know that Ganesh had not returned home at night? If he had been found earlier, he could have been taken to the hospital and saved."

Jothi finished her coffee in silence. She wiped her mouth, removed her hair towel and spread it on the railings of the cot. Perhaps, I had raised an insensitive question. Before I could make amends, she said,

"If yesterday was the first time that he had returned late, I would have searched for him. It was a daily routine. Ever since the temple festival was announced last week, he had had a gala time. I had sat up all night and gone to sleep when the cock crowed. I have not slept in the night for a year now."

I clasped her turmeric tinted hands in silence.

"He was really fond of you," she continued.

"And I really loved him," she added.

"Young men are unpredictable. Which young man would stay at home after the village festival is announced? If you started counting the wives of men from the southern districts, who have slept peacefully, it would not even be a hand count," said Kamatchi Patti from the door way.

"Patti, don't give that excuse. Things have to change with time. Go to sleep."

Night crept in like a blanket between Jothi and me. She slept on the floor with her hand tucked in like a pillow. Looking at her, I too drifted off. When distant relatives came at dawn, there were more tears.

"Jothi, shall we have coffee?"

Jothi was fast asleep. Her face was serene like that of a new born baby. Her right hand was holding the baby bump protectively. Perhaps, after one whole year, she had slept peacefully only yesterday. She breathed steadily and was motionless like a sculpture. Her lips were slightly parted in a smile. I got up, closed the door and laid down again, so that she wouldn't be disturbed.

Glossary

Aatha: literally means mother but used to refer to a woman

Akka: elder sister

Ambarai: small container with compartments

Amma: mother

Anna/Annachi/Annan: elder brother

Appa: father

Atchadai: consecrated yellow rice

Ayyo: Tamil word used to denote a variety of emotions including surprise, sorrow, fear and regret

Chenthurukka dabba: casket shaped holder for vermilion
Chinnamma: younger aunt
Chitappa: younger uncle
Chutney: thick sauce used extensively in Indian cuisine
Cooum River: name of the river flowing through Chennai, which is highly polluted
Dhoti: a traditional garment worn around the waist by men in India
Dupatta: a stole like garment
Edupatta payalugala: Scallywags
Jamakkaalam: a thick and heavy rug used as a carpet
Kadambam: a colourful string of mixed flowers
Kapi: coffee
Kalavanl mazhai: stealthy rain
Karisal: refers to the type of soil in the districts of Madurai and Ramanathapuram. More broadly, it refers to nativity or the native touch

Karupatti: palm jaggery
Kittipul: tip cat game
Kumbabhishekam: renovation and consecration of a temple
Kumkum: vermilion
Kutty: young one
Mama: uncle
Manni: sister in law
Maruthani/Mehendi: temporary body art made from staining the leaves of hyssop plant
Muttu Veedu: birthing hut; a separate enclosure for delivery of the child
Neecha thanni: fermented rice water
Paati: grandmother
Padappai: making hay stacks
Pallu: top folds of a sari
Pappa: infant
Pechiyatha: a goddess in the local traditions
Periamma: elder aunt
Pirandai: veld grape
Pottu: the vermilion mark on the forehead
Rasam: spiced pepper soup

Rasumagan: literally, Rasu's son. It is an accepted practice to address an individual by their relationship
Rattha poriyal: a delicacy made out of fried goat's blood seasoned with spices
Sambar: stew made of lentils and vegetables
Sannadhi theru: street circumscribing a temple
Sharara: loose pleated trousers
Sungudi sari: a special cotton sari with traditional tie and dye prints made in the city of Madurai
Thangachi: younger sister
Thali: chain worn by a married Hindu woman
Thayi: literally means mother but a reference to any woman
Theetu: unclean; refers to the perceived impurity of menstrual blood and in places of mourning
Thinai: the fivefold classification of landscape in sangam eco-poetics and its attendant flora, fauna, emotions and feelings

Thombi: implies thambi, meaning younger brother
Velliyam: an alloy of tin
Zari: artistic thread work woven mainly in silk

Some of our widely acclaimed translations that may interest readers are:

Lamps in the Whirlpool (Tamil), *Sasi is Waiting and Other Stories* (Tamil), *In Defiance: Our Stories* (Tamil), *Relive Indira Goswami* (Assamese), *Before the Break of Dawn: Secrets of Namboodiri Women* (Malayalam), *The Areca Nut Tree and Other Stories* (Assamese), *Jangam: A forgotten exodus in which thousands died* (Assamese), *Bengal Famine: An Unpunished Genocide* (Bangla) and *Ramayana: A Comparative Study of Ramakathas* (Tamil), *Manhunt* (Malayalam), *Reliving Tagore* (Bangla), *Reliving Sujatha* (Tamil), *Ashapurna Devi through her stories* (Bangla).

RAJAM KRISHNAN
Lamps in the Whirlpool
Translated from Tamil by
Uma Narayanan | Prema Seetharam

Sasi is waiting
AND OTHER STORIES BY SUJATHA

IN DEFIANCE
OUR STORIES

Relive
INDIRA
GOSWAMI
The Rich Legacy Of Her Stories

Before
the Break
of Dawn
Secrets of the Namboodiri Women
Devaki Nilayamgode

THE
ARECA
NUT
TREE
AND
OTHER
STORIES
Contemporary
Women's Writing
from Assam

RELIVING DEBENDRANATH ACHARYA
JANGAM
A forgotten
exodus
in which
thousands died
AWARD WINNER
Translated by Amit R Baishya

Bengal
Famine
An Unpunished
Genocide
A Commentary on
SYAMA PRASAD MOOKERJEE'S
Panchasher Manwantar

RAMAYANA
A Comparative Study of Ramakathas
A A MANAVALAN

RUMA CHAKRAVARTI
Reliving
TAGORE
Poetry, Prose and Perceptions

MANHUNT
Seashore Saga of the
Punnapra-Vayalar Uprising
Saga of a desperate uprising crushed by ruthless authority that reverberates into the present. Written with empathy and understanding. A must-read.
—Adoor Gopalakrishnan, film-maker
KV MOHANKUMAR
translated by Manjula Cherkil
VAYALAR
RAMAVARMA
AWARD
Vitasta

RUMA CHAKRAVARTI
THE
MYSTERY
THAT IS
WOMAN
Ashapurna Devi
through her stories

Vitasta
translated by Vimala Balakrishnan
Reliving
SUJATHA
His best stories in English